# Bedtime Stories for the Very Young

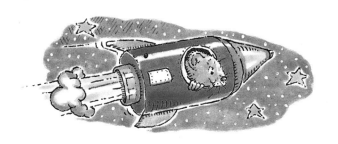

For Gina  S.G.
For Jannie  C.F.

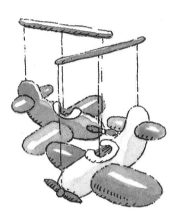

Kingfisher Books, Grisewood & Dempsey Ltd,
Elsley House, 24–30 Great Titchfield Street, London W1P 7AD

First published in 1991 by Kingfisher Books

2 4 6 8 10 9 7 5 3

BRITISH LIBRARY CATALOGUING IN PUBLICATION DATA
Grindley, Sally
Bedtime stories for the very young.
I. Title    II. Fisher, Chris
823.914[J]
ISBN 086272 779 0

Designed by Tony Potter
Phototypeset by Tradespools Ltd, Frome
Colour separations by Scantrans Pte Ltd, Singapore
Printed and bound in Italy

# Bedtime Stories for the Very Young

Selected and edited by
SALLY GRINDLEY

Illustrated by
CHRIS FISHER

Kingfisher Books

# Contents

# Emily Hogg and Doctor Dog Go to the Ceiling

## SUE LIMB

"Goodnight, my little egg," said Emily's Dad, and then he made a whistling sound: CHEWP CHEWP CHEWP TIRILEE.

"Goodnight, Big Bird," said Emily.

Emily was in a bird phase right now. Even her pyjama top had a pattern of yellow birds.

After her Dad had gone, Emily lay and looked at the ceiling. Up there above her head was a strange stain. Sometimes it looked like a lake, sometimes like an island. Sometimes it looked like a tree, and sometimes like an angry old man.

"What does that stain look like to you?" asked Emily. In bed with her was Doctor Dog – her cuddliest, oldest toy.

"Wow! It looks just like a bone!" he barked. "Let's go and see! Hold tight for take-off!"

There was a whirring sound, and Emily's bed rose up in the air as if it was a helicopter. Emily held on tight and watched her bedroom get smaller and further away, until the window was the size of a tiny fingernail.

"Ladies 'n' Gentlemen," announced Doctor Dog, flying the bedicopter very expertly into a wild blue wind, "you may unfasten your seatbelts."

Up ahead Emily saw a glittering lake getting bigger and bigger as they went towards it.

"Ah!" said Emily, "so it *is* a lake!"

In the middle of the lake was a tiny island.

"Oh no, it's an island after all!"

In the middle of the island was a tree.

"I see!" said Emily, "so it really is a *tree*! Can we land on that island, Doctor Dog?"

"Going in to land now," reported Doctor Dog. "Thirty . . . twenty . . . We have landed. A giant leap for dog kind." And he bounded out and frisked under the tree.

"Wow! What a great place! Throw me a stick, Emily!"

Emily wasn't so sure. There was something about the place that seemed sad. It was so silent and still. All the same, she reached up into the tree, broke off a little stick and threw it for Doctor Dog, way out into the lake. He plunged in after it. Everything seemed even quieter after he'd gone.

Emily looked into the tree, and saw some green apples hanging there. She picked up one and sat down on a rock to eat it. But the first bite was so sour and awful, she threw it away into the lake. It made a sad PLOP sound which echoed into the stillness. Then suddenly a voice crackled out, sharp and deep.

"You steal my apples and then you throw them away! What sort of girl are you?"

Emily couldn't see anybody. Then, all at once, she noticed two black eyes shining from the trunk of the tree. Yes, the tree had a face – the face of an angry old man. Its branches were his arms and its twigs were his knotty fingers.

"I'm very sorry," Emily said. "We'll go away. I'll just call my dog." Doctor Dog bounded from the lake and shook himself, all over the trunk of the tree.

"Dogs!" snapped the tree man. "I hate 'em! And he's got one of my sticks in his mouth."

"I'm sorry," said Emily.

"Who are you talking to, Emily," barked Doctor Dog.

"It's the tree!" whispered Emily. "Give his stick back – he's very angry." Doctor Dog tried to walk towards the tree, but he couldn't move.

"Hey!" he whined, "I'm rooted to the ground."

So was Emily. And so was the bedicopter. The tree's roots had wound themselves around their feet, and all around Emily's bed.

"You'll never get away!" cried the tree-man. "I'll keep you here. Then I won't be lonely any more."

Doctor Dog started to howl, and Emily was very near crying. Then she had an idea.

"I know why you're lonely!" she said. "Because you've got no birds! That's what a tree needs – birds!" And she pulled off her pyjama top. "Look!" she went on, "my pyjama top is covered with birds!" And she threw the pyjama top towards the tree.

As it flew, there was a sort of golden explosion and all the little yellow birds burst out of it in a brilliant cloud. They twittered and fluttered and perched on the branches of the tree.

"Cheep cheep cheep TIRILEE!"

Some began to build nests. Some sharpened their beaks on the branches. Suddenly the great green tree was full of music and life, and a slow grin spread across its gnarled old face. The roots uncoiled themselves from around Emily's ankles. She was free! And so were Doctor Dog and the bedicopter. Quickly waving

10

goodbye to the smiling tree, they took off and flew back home.

"Emily," said Emily's mother next day, "where's your pyjama top?"

"Oh," Emily began to explain, "you see the stain on the ceiling? Well, it's an old man, but he's a tree really, and he lives on an island, in the middle of a lake, and he needed the birds because he was so lonely, so I gave him my pyjama top."

"Well, that's a great story," said her mother, "but where's your pyjama top *really*?"

Emily sighed. There were some things grown-ups just didn't understand. Her mother went on looking for that pyjama top for a week and a day, even though Emily kept on telling her it was on the ceiling – and come to think of it, if you looked up at the stain, you could see the pyjama top clear as anything, along with the lake and the island and the old tree-man. And if the wind was in the right direction, you could even hear the birds sing.

# Ella's Bedtime Story

## LEON ROSSELSON

"Ella," called Michael.

"I'm asleep," said Ella and gave a loud snore.

"I can't sleep," said Michael. "The wind's blowing noises in my ears."

"You wanted to go camping," said Ella.

"The ground's hard," complained Michael. "And there are slugs everywhere."

"No there aren't," said Ella. "You're just imagining."

"Tell me a story," Michael said in a song-song voice.

Ella groaned. "You tell me a story for a change."

"But you're supposed to look after me when Mum and Dad aren't here."

"Who says?"

"Mum says. Look after Michael, she says, 'cos he's only little." Michael giggled.

Ella stared at the roof of their little tent. "I'm never going to be a mum," she said.

"You'll have to be," said Michael. "You're a girl."

"I will not," said Ella.

"Well, what will you be when you grow up?"

Ella thought. "A juggler," she said, finally.

"You can't juggle."

"Who says?"

"I've never seen you juggle. When have you ever juggled?"

"You'd be surprised," Ella said mysteriously.

"I'm going to be an elephant-tamer," said Michael.

"Humph," said Ella. "I've never seen you tame elephants."

"You'd be surprised," sang Michael and laughed.

"In a circus?"

"Everywhere. Wherever there's an elephant to tame, they'll send for me because only I know the magic word."

"What magic word?"

"Sausages! And when the elephant hears that word, he'll stop stamping his feet and throwing people about and he'll kneel in front of me and – "

"What?"

"Be tamed."

"A likely story," said Ella.

"Suffering sausages," Michael said. "Your turn."

"Once upon a time – "

"Not a fairy story," groaned Michael.

"Once upon a time," Ella insisted, "there was a little girl called Ella."

"Your name's Ella," said Michael.

"So it is," she said. "Well, this girl, Ella, lived in a castle with her Mum and Dad and little brother and she was, everybody thought, the most beautiful girl in the world."

"Humph," said Michael.

"It's my story," said Ella.

"I only said 'humph'," said Michael, putting his thumb in his mouth.

"The most beautiful girl in the world," Ella repeated. "Everyone wanted to marry her. But she wasn't interested in marrying because what she most wanted was to juggle.

"'You can't juggle,' said her Dad. 'You only have to get out of bed to trip over the carpet. How can you juggle?'

"'You can't juggle,' said her Mum. 'You only have to sit at the breakfast table to upset a bowl of cornflakes. How can you juggle?'

"'You can't juggle,' said her little brother. 'I only have to throw a ball for you to drop it. How can you juggle?'

"But Ella was stubborn. 'I will juggle,' she said to herself. And she took three ripe plums from the plum tree and threw them into the air. Split, splat, splot. Three squashed plums lying on the earth. So she picked three red apples from the apple tree and tried juggling with those. Biff, baff, boff. Three bruised apples lying on the grass. But she wouldn't give up. She tried with stones. She tried with sticks. She tried with tennis balls. She tried with footballs. She tried with hats, shoes, bricks, weetabix, chocolate drops, cherry stones, lollipops and bars of soap. Once she tried with her Mum's best teacups. Crish, crash, crosh. Bits of china all over the kitchen floor. Was her Mum cross! But it was no good. She couldn't juggle. Poor Ella. She was very sad. And even being the most beautiful girl in the world didn't make up for it.

"One day, the doorbell rang."

"Ding-dong," said Michael from his sleeping bag.

"'Who's that?' said her Mum.

"'I expect it's just someone wanting to marry me,' said Ella. 'It usually is.' She was practising juggling with three balls of wool. That's all she was allowed to juggle with now so she couldn't do any more damage.

"'Go and answer it, then,' said her Mum. 'You and your juggling. It's about time you did something useful. Why when I was your age –'

"But Ella was off down the long stairway that led to the castle door.

"The bell rang again."

"Ding-dong," said Michael.

"Ella opened the door. There in front of her was the strangest-looking little man she'd ever seen. He had blue hair, a perfectly round face that shone like the sun, eyes as bright as silver and rainbow-coloured clothes.

"'Are you the most beautiful girl in the world?' he asked.

"'That's me,' said Ella.

"'I've come from far away to see you,' said the man.

"'Where's far away?' asked Ella.

"'High, high in the sky and over the moon,' replied the man. 'And now at last I've seen you, I can return to my own home and tell everybody I've seen –'

"'Yes, yes,' said Ella. 'But can you teach me to juggle?'

"'Of course,' he said. And reaching into the air, he plucked out a ball.

"'What colour is this?' he asked.

"'Orange,' said Ella.

"'Like the sun,' said the strange man. And reaching into the air, he plucked out another ball.

"'Blue,' said Ella.

"'Like the moon,' said the man.

"Ella frowned. 'The moon isn't blue,' she said.

"'It is where I come from,' he said. Then he reached up and drew out a third ball.

"'Silver,' said Ella.

16

"'Like the morning star. Throw those into the air and they will soar and swoop and circle and spin but they will never fall to earth.' And he handed the balls to Ella.

"'Thank you,' she said. 'Will you stay for tea?'

"But he was gone.

"Ella looked doubtfully at the three balls. Orange, blue and silver. She took the orange ball and threw it high into the air. Then the blue ball. Then the silver ball. They soared and swooped and circled and span down into her hands and up again, soaring and swooping and circling and spinning; but never, never did they fall to earth.

"Her father saw her as he came home from work. 'Wonder of wonders,' he said. 'Our Ella's juggling.'

"Her mother came running from the castle kitchen. 'Wonder of wonders,' she said. 'Our Ella can juggle.'

"Her brother came racing from the castle garden. 'Wonder of wonders,' he said. 'Our Ella's a juggler.'

"And, with the balls still soaring and swooping and circling and spinning over her head, Ella skipped out of the castle and down the hill and into the village square, where she made the orange and silver and blue balls dance brilliant patterns in the sky while the crowds of people watched and wondered and told each other that they had never, in all their born days, seen juggling like it."

There was a long silence.

"Michael," called Ella quietly.

But there was no reply from his sleeping bag; Michael was asleep.

Ella, snuggling deep into her own sleeping bag, listened to the quietness of the night. Beyond the curving roof of the tent, she thought she could see the round moon shining. If she stood up and reached out, she would be able to touch the moon. She saw herself growing tall and reaching out and touching the moon and then unhooking it from the sky and sending it soaring and spinning into space. Then she reached out again and unpacked the stars and made them dance like jewelled lightning across the dark face of the sky. All this she saw as she closed her eyes until she, too, was lulled and lost in a sleep of dreams.

# Fussy

## ANNE FINE

Fussy was tired. His eyes were drooping and his thumb kept creeping into his mouth. But before he could go to bed he had to find his special yellow blanket.

And then he needed Elephant with his big flappy ears, in case he was lonely.

And then he needed the huge, shiny picture book you could wipe clean, in case he wanted to look at the pictures.

And he wanted his mobile aeroplanes spinning round and round above his head – No! He wanted them stopped.

And then Fussy wanted some water in the cup with the top with the little holes, in case he was thirsty.

And he wanted the fat round pebble he found on the beach one day.

And he wanted the curtains closed so he couldn't see the creepy, wavy branches on the tree outside the window –

No! He wanted them open so he *could* see the creepy,

wavy branches on the tree outside the window.

And he wanted his family of pink rabbits, and all his furry glove puppets, and his bright wooden bricks.

And he wanted his light off –

No! He wanted his light back on again.

And he wanted his telephone with the long, red loopy wire, and his sailing boat, and his zoo animals, and the shiny winter jacket Gran bought him on Saturday, and his green plastic frog, and his truck and his toy cars, and his pretend bottle of beer.

And then, at last, everything was *just right*. It was exactly how he wanted it. So Fussy shut his eyes and fell asleep.

PHEW!

He slept for two whole hours. First he rolled all the way over. Then he rolled all the way back. Then he kicked about a bit.

So the rabbit family got all mixed up with the furry glove puppets. And the bright wooden bricks fell into the back of the truck. And the long, red loopy wire of the telephone tangled in the boat's sails. And the toy cars slid down the sleeves of the shiny winter jacket Gran bought him on Saturday. And the fat round pebble he found on the beach one day knocked over the huge,

shiny picture book you could wipe clean, so it fell on the green plastic frog. And water dripped out of the holes in the top of the cup onto the heads of all the animals from his zoo.

And Elephant nearly disappeared completely under the yellow blanket with the pretend bottle of beer . . .

What a mess! What a *terrible* mess! It certainly wasn't just right any more. It wasn't how Fussy wanted it at all.

But when he woke up, did he mind? No. Not a bit!

You see he wasn't fussy any more. He'd had his nap!

# The Lamb Who Couldn't Sleep

### JOHN YEOMAN

It was Springtime on the marshes, and every day the young lambs raced around the fields and jumped and turned in the air. Every evening, they settled down beside their mothers, out of the wind, and fell fast asleep.

All except one.

He could never get to sleep at the right time. Instead, he would lie awake listening to the snores coming from all the other sheep in the field. No matter how hard he tried, he just didn't seem to be able to fall asleep. What was worse, just as the first faint light of the sun began to appear over the hedge and the mist began to clear from the field, he would start to doze off.

Every morning began the same way.

"Time to get up," said his mother. "It's going to be a lovely morning. Have a little drink and nibble some fresh grass and then you can go off and play with your friends."

Through his sleepy, half-opened eyes, the lamb could see some of his friends already at their leaping and spinning around the field.

"I don't think I want to play yet," he said, and gave a big yawn.

"Oh dear," said his mother. "Didn't you sleep very well?"

"No," he said. "I didn't sleep at all. I never do."

"Why don't you try counting sheep tonight?" his mother suggested.

That night he took his mother's advice. As he snuggled down beside her, sheltered from the breeze, he began to count. Because he was a very young lamb he could only count up to three, but he thought that counting up to three over and over again was probably as good as counting up to a hundred once.

"One, two, THREE ... one, two, THREE ... one, two, THREE ... one, two, THREE."

"What does that young idiot think he's doing?" came the voice of a sheep out of the darkness.

"Sounds like he's starting a race," came a reply.

"Is he trying to get us to join in a song?" suggested another.

"I think you're keeping the others awake," his mother whispered. "That's enough counting for tonight."

The lamb just sighed, rested his chin on his front feet, and settled down to another sleepless night.

After breakfast the next morning he staggered across the field to say hello to his friends. But his eyes were so

bleary and his legs were so unsteady that he stumbled right into a big oak tree.

"It isn't good manners to go bumping into people's homes like that," said a voice from above.

The lamb looked up and saw an owl sitting on a branch.

"I'm very sorry," said the lamb. "I'm so tired that I didn't see the tree."

"How can you be tired?" snapped the owl. "You haven't done anything yet!"

"I didn't sleep. I never do."

"Deary me," said the owl, in a softer voice. "We shall have to do something about that. Come back to see me this afternoon, and I'll give you some of my special sleeping mixture."

"Oh, thank you," said the lamb.

And he set off to join his friends, feeling much better already.

Back at the oak tree after lunch, he was a little disappointed to find that the owl hadn't been able to make his special sleeping mixture.

"It's nearly ready," the bird explained, "but I'm afraid I'm short of one or two items. Would you be good enough to bring me a feather which has dropped from a crow, please? That fellow over there has a loose one sticking out, do you see?"

The lamb raced after the crow, which waited until he was near before flying up and landing a few feet away. The lamb gave chase again and the crow did exactly the same thing. It happened again and again, until finally the feather came free and fluttered to the ground.

Quick as a flash the lamb picked it up in his mouth and ran back to the tree.

"Well done," said the owl. "Just leave it there while you go for the other thing."

"You mean there's more?" panted the lamb.

"Well, you want the mixture to work properly, don't you?" asked the owl. Yes, the lamb certainly wanted to mixture to work properly.

"Good," said the owl. "Now, you see that black lamb over there? He's got a particular kind of thistle sticking

to his fleece. Just bring me that, and then we're ready."

The lamb bounded off again. When the black lamb saw him coming, he thought it was a game and raced away as fast as he could. They ran and ran, this way and that across the field, for ages and ages – until finally the thistle dropped off and the lamb was able to pick it up.

He returned to the tree, all hot and puffed out.

"That's exactly what we need," said the owl. "Unfortunately, it's too late this afternoon to finish making the mixture. But you shall have it tomorrow. Go back to your mother now."

It was getting dark when the lamb got back to his mother.

"Had a nice afternoon?" she asked.

And do you know, he was so worn out that he just lay down and fell asleep.

The next morning he was completely refreshed from his good night's sleep and couldn't wait to tell the owl.

"I slept soundly all night!" he said.

"I thought you might," said the owl, with a wink. "So you won't be needing my mixture after all. You see, it's my belief that you'll sleep well every night from now on."

And the wise old owl was right. The lamb spent every day chasing around with his friends, and every night he fell sound asleep as soon as he closed his eyes.

And I hope you do, too.

# Watch Out for Tusker

## SARAH HAYES

Tess stared crossly at the raindrops making rivers on her window pane. She didn't want to play inside. Her room was a mess. Tess kicked a brick under the bed. Clonk! The brick hit something that wasn't the wall. Tess knelt down to have a look, and then she remembered the toy-box Dad had fetched from the loft. His old cars were in there, all scratched and battered. Tess had pushed the box under her bed and forgotten about it. Now she pulled it out.

The box was heavy. She took off the lid and looked inside. The cars weren't very interesting, but there were other things underneath, done up in tissue paper. Tess unwrapped one of the packages: it was a painted metal horse with big feet. It wasn't scratched or battered like the cars. Tess weighed the horse in her hand. It was heavier than the animals you get nowadays. She unwrapped another package. Five ducklings fell on to the carpet. Tess had found Dad's old farm.

There were horses and cows and sheep and lambs and dogs and cats and ducks and chickens and a turkey and lots of pigs, all different kinds. Tess liked the big black pig with the squashed-in face. There were people too, and an old-fashioned tractor with a trailer and hay bales you could take out. At the very bottom of the box Tess found a farmhouse with roses painted on it and real curtains.

It took a long time to set the farm out properly. Tess was about to put the cars back into the box when she noticed a small package she had missed. Inside was a dull brown pig with a long snout. She put it with the other pigs.

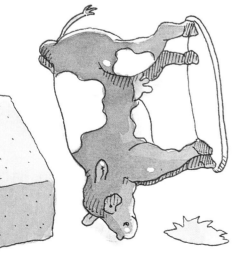

Dad was late that night and Tess was almost asleep when he came in to say good night.

"Look at your farm, Dad," said Tess.

"I've just been looking at it," said Dad. "That was Grandad's farm before it was mine. It's yours now; you take good care of it." Then Dad said something very peculiar: "WATCH OUT FOR TUSKER." At least that's what Tess thought he said.

The sun was shining when Tess woke up. She looked at the farm sitting in the middle of her messy room. Then she jumped out of bed. Something was wrong! She knelt down. Everything was wrong! The ducks were all huddled together in the sheep field, and the sheep were in the trailer. A cow was on its side on the farmhouse doorstep and the lady with the milking stool was lying on her back with her legs in the air. The chickens and the turkey had disappeared. Only the pigs were unchanged. They stood peacefully in their field just where Tess had left them. Their gate was slightly open and the dull brown pig was poking his long snout through the gap. Tess closed the gate and put the brown pig in the pigsty.

She found the chickens and the turkey under the tractor trailer. It almost looked as though they were hiding.

Tess put everything back the way it had been before. "You be good," she said. Then she went to find Nicky

32

who lived next door. Nicky was older than Tess. He loved the farm. He built a haystack with the hay bales, and he showed Tess how to make a pond for the ducks out of kitchen foil.

Dad was very impressed with the new pond.

"Something happened last night," said Tess. "Something very bad." Dad shook his head. Then he said it again: "WATCH OUT FOR TUSKER."

"What do you mean?" demanded Tess. "Who is Tusker?"

"I don't know," said Dad. "It's something Grandad used to say to me."

Next morning, when Tess woke up, it had happened again, only worse. The bales from Nicky's haystack were all over the place and the trailer was tipped on its end. The big horses were upside-down in the duck pond and the foil was ripped. The cows and the sheep were crammed into the farmhouse, all on top of each other, and the people lay face down in the barn. The ducks and the chickens were on the farmhouse roof and the turkey was perched on the chimney. Fences and gates were everywhere.

"At least the pigs are all right," said Mum cheerfully. And so they were – in their field just where Tess had left them. But their gate was wide open, and the brown pig with the long snout was not in his sty. He was halfway across the sheep field.

"You are a bad pig," said Tess. She picked him up and looked at him curiously. "I didn't know pigs had tusks," she said. Then she remembered Dad's words – WATCH OUT FOR TUSKER.

"Let me have a look," said Mum. Tess handed her the dull brown pig with the long snout. "That's not a pig!" said Mum. "That's a wild boar. Wild boars don't live on farms: they're dangerous!"

Tess couldn't wait for Dad to come home. When she heard Dad's key in the front door, she rushed to meet him.

"I've found him!" she shouted.

"Found who?" said Dad, who was putting down his things.

"Tusker," said Tess. She opened her hand, and showed Dad the pig with the long snout and tusks. "Grandad's wild boar."

"Good heavens!" said Dad. He sat down at the kitchen table rather heavily. "Watch out for Tusker," he said almost to himself. "WATCH OUT FOR TUSKER," he said again a bit louder.

"He wasn't happy on the farm," said Tess.

"He wouldn't be," said Dad. "Tusker is a wild creature. He was probably frightened of all those gates and fences and machines and people."

At the bottom of the garden there was an overgrown patch that Mum and Dad called their wild garden. That was where Tess and Dad took Tusker. Tess put him gently down under an ivy leaf.

"Goodbye, Tusker," she said.

"Goodbye, Tusker," said Dad.

Next morning Tess woke up to find her farm exactly as she had left it. But Tusker had disappeared from under the ivy leaf. They never saw him again, but Tess was sure he was happy in the wild garden. And if ever anything went wrong – if a plant fell over, or a cabbage got nibbled, or a flowerpot got broken, someone was sure to say: WATCH OUT FOR TUSKER.

# The King of the Blue Lagoon

## ANN TURNBULL

When Sally was at the seaside she found a stone on the beach. It was grey and oval and smoothed by the waves and it just filled the palm of her hand. Sally knew at once that it was a magic stone. She kept it in her pocket.

One day when Sally was skipping in the school playground the stone bounced out of her pocket and fell – plop! – into a puddle.

The puddle changed. It changed from a grey rainy-day puddle to a pool of deep, deep blue, with pink rocks in it, and glinting fish that flicked between them. Sally heard the boom and hiss of the surf. She put her hand into the water. It was warm and she felt a tickle of fish.

Her stone lay at the bottom. Sally took it out, and at once the blue sea, the surf, the pink rocks and glinting fish all vanished. And from Sally's hand came a voice that sighed,

"Far from the coral caves
Far from the sea
A witch's magic has enchanted me."

Sally put the stone back in her pocket. She looked around. No one else had noticed.

When she got home she took the stone into the garden. In the garden was a pond, with rocks around the edge and a plastic gnome fishing at the side.

Sally put the stone into the pond.

The water turned deep, deep blue, the rocks became a coral reef, the gnome turned into a mermaid who combed her hair and sang wild songs.

Sally took the stone out.

The blue sea, the coral reef and the mermaid all vanished and Sally heard a voice that sighed,

"Far from the coral caves

Far from the sea

A witch's magic has enchanted me."

That night, Sally put the stone into her bath.

The bath water turned deep, deep blue. The bath foam turned to sea foam. The soap became an angel fish. The flannel became a manta ray. An island with palm trees grew out of the soap dish. On Sally's plastic boat a pirate crew hoisted the Jolly Roger. Sally launched a Spanish galleon, laden with gold. There was a battle and cannon boomed across the water.

And all the time the stone lay at the bottom of the bath and Sally's mother hadn't noticed anything.

Sally took the stone out. At once the blue sea, the angel fish, the Spaniards and pirates all vanished and

she heard a voice that sighed,

"Far from the coral caves

Far from the sea

A witch's magic has enchanted me."

After that, Sally always put the stone into her bath. But although the water changed and the boats changed and the soap and soap dish changed, the stone never changed. It lay on the bottom, cold and sad, and when Sally took it out, it always sighed,

"Far from the coral caves

Far from the sea

A witch's magic has enchanted me."

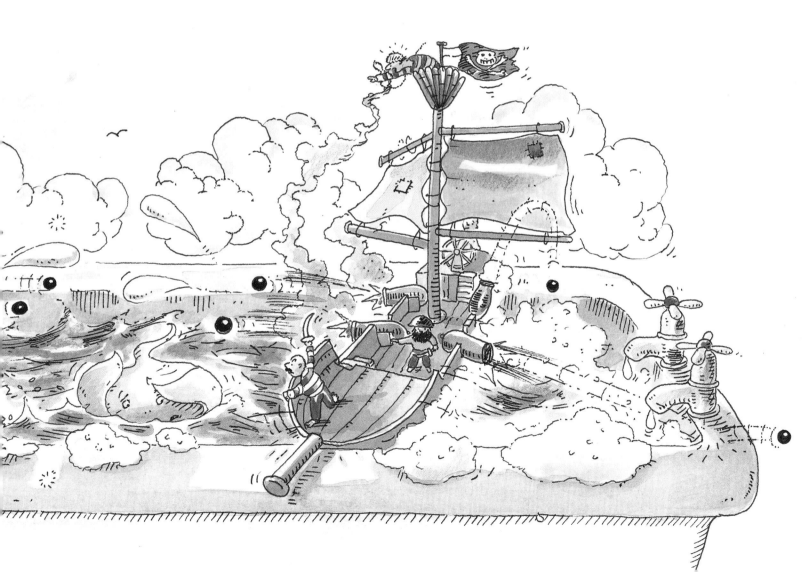

One day Sally went to the seaside again. She took the stone with her.

Sally waded into the sea, holding the stone in her cupped hands. She squatted, and the sea washed over the stone and rocked it against her fingers.

The sea was a grey, cold sea. Sally thought it would change, but it didn't. Nothing changed. The sea was grey; the rocks were grey; the sky was grey.

But suddenly, in Sally's hands, the stone came alive. It twitched. It wiggled. It slithered and slipped. Sally looked down and saw that the stone had changed to a fish: a bright, bright fish with a rose-red body and turquoise stripes, golden eyes with black rims, fins that flicked silver and a rose-red shimmering tail. On its head was a crown.

"Oh!" said Sally. She was so surprised that she opened her fingers and the fish slipped through.

Before she could catch it, it flicked its tail and wiggled

its body and swam away, bright as a jewel in the grey sea. Sally watched it grow smaller, and smaller, until at last it was no bigger than a sequin. Then it disappeared.

Sally felt something scraping and bumping against her foot. She bent down and picked up a shell. It was a big shell, pale pink and spiralled, that looked as if it had come from a blue sea far away.

Sally waded back to the shore, holding her shell. She knew at once that it was a magic shell. She showed it to her mother.

"You can hear the sea in a shell," said Sally's mother.

Sally held the shell to her ear. She heard the sea. She heard the boom and hiss of far-off surf. And above the sound of the surf she heard a glad voice, singing:

"Deep in the coral caves
Under the sea
King of the blue lagoon now I am free."

# Norty Boy

## DICK KING-SMITH

Hylda was an old-fashioned sort of animal. She did not hold with the free and easy ways of the modern hedgehog, and even preferred to call herself by the old name of 'hedgepig'. She planned to bring up her seven hedgepiglets very strictly.

'Children should be seen and not heard' was one of her favourite sayings, and 'Speak when you're spoken to' was another. She taught them to say 'Please' and 'Thank you', to eat nicely, to sniff quietly if their noses were running, and never to scratch in public, no matter how many fleas they had.

Six of them – three boys and three girls – grew up to be well-behaved, with beautiful manners, but the seventh was a great worry to Hylda and her husband Herbert. This seventh hedgepiglet was the despair of Hylda's life. He was not only seen but constantly heard, speaking whether he was spoken to or not, and he never said 'Please' or 'Thank you'. He gobbled his food in a revoltingly slobbery way, he sniffed very loudly indeed and he was forever scratching.

His real name was Norton, but he was more often known as Norty.

Now some mother animals can wallop their young ones if they do not do what they are told. A lioness can cuff her cub, a monkey can clip its child round the ear, or an elephant can give her baby a biff with her trunk. But it's not so easy for hedgehogs.

"Sometimes," said Hylda to Herbert. "I wish that hedgepigs didn't have prickles"

"Why is that, my dear?" said Herbert.

"Because then I could give our Norty a good hiding. He deserves it."

"Why is that, my dear?" said Herbert.

"Not only is he disobedient, he has taken to answering me back. Why can't he be good like the others? Never have I known such a hedgepiglet. I shall be glad when November comes."

"Why is that, my dear?" said Herbert.

"Because then it's time to hibernate, of course, and we can all have a good sleep. For five blissful months I shall not have to listen to that impudent, squeaky little voice arguing, complaining, refusing to do what I say and generally giving me cheek."

Hylda should have known it would not be that easy.

When November came, she said to her husband and the seven children, "Come along, all of you."

"Yes, Mummy," said the three good boys and the

three good girls, and "Why is that, my dear?" said
Herbert, but Norty only said, "Shan't."

"Norty," said Hylda. "If you do not do what you are
told, I shall get your father to give you a good hard
smack."

Norty fluffed up his spines and sniggered.

"You'll be sorry if you do, Dad," he said.

"Where are we going, Mummy?" asked one of the
hedgepiglets.

"We are going to find a nice deep bed of dry leaves,
where we can hibernate."

"What does 'hibernate' mean, Mummy?" asked
another.

"It means to go to sleep, all through the winter. When it's rainy and blowy and frosty and snowy outside, we shall all be fast asleep under the leaf pile, all cosy and warm. Won't that be lovely?"

"No," said Norty.

"Norton!" said his mother angrily. "Are you coming or are you not?"

"No," said Norty.

"Oh well, stay here then!" snapped Hylda. "And freeze to death!" and she trotted off with the rest.

In a far corner of the garden they found a nice deep bed of dry leaves, and Hylda and Herbert and the six good hedgepiglets burrowed their way into it, and curled up tight, and shut their eyes, and went to sleep.

The following April they woke up, and opened their eyes, and uncurled, and burrowed out into the Spring sunshine.

"Goodbye Mummy! Goodbye Daddy!" chorused the six good hedgepiglets, and off they trotted to seek their fortunes.

"Oh Herbert!" said Hylda. "I feel so sad."

"Why is that, my dear?" said Herbert.

"I should never have left our Norty out in the cold last November. He will have frozen to death, poor little fellow. What does it matter that he was rude and disobedient and cheeky? Oh, if only I could hear his squeaky voice again, I'd be the happiest hedgepig ever!"

At that moment there was a rustling from the other side of the bed of leaves, and out came Norty.

"Can't you keep your voices down?" he said, yawning. "A fellow can't get a wink of sleep."

"Oh Norty!" cried Hylda. "Come and give Mummy a kiss!"

"Shan't," said Norty.

"Aren't you pleased to see us?"

"No," said Norty.

At this Hylda completely lost her temper.

"Well, push off then!" she shouted. "Your brothers and sisters have all gone, so get lost!"

"Shan't," said Norty. "I'm going to stay with you, so there!"

"Oh no, you're not!" screamed Hylda. "You're the rudest hedgepig in the world and your father's the most boring, and I've had enough of both of you!" and she ran away as fast as she could go.

Herbert and Norty stared after her. Norty scratched his fleas and sniffed very noisily.

"Looks like she's done a bunk, Dad," he said.

"Yes," said Herbert. "Why is that, my dear?"

"Can't think," said Norty. "But then she always was prickly."

# A Dragon's Bedtime

## JUDY HINDLEY

Long, long ago – before your grandmother was born, before cities were built, before there were even any people in the world – a family of dragons began their dragon day.

"Eat up," said Daryll's mum. "You need your breakfast. It's going to be a long day for you."

You've probably heard people talk about having a long day. You may have wondered what on earth they mean. Well, when Daryll's mum said 'long', she meant LONG. A dragon's day is not an ordinary day. The day of a dragon lasts for seven thousand YEARS.

Imagine playing for seven thousand years, without a nap!

Of course, to a dragon, it seems different. To a dragon, normal days come and go, blip, blip, blip! Like a light going on and off, on and off. Between the blips of daytime, stars wheel and flicker and go out again, like bursts of fireworks. Whole years go by very quickly, blowing hot and cold as the summers turn to winters. It would seem very peculiar to you and me but, to a dragon, this is just the way things are.

Today, however, Daryll was rather nervous. It was going to be a special day for him – his first day on his own without his parents.

To look at him you might not have guessed, but in fact, Daryll was just a baby. Though he was tall as a church and long as a football field, he was only young and small, as dragons go. "What shall I DO?" he whimpered, clinging to his mother. (You can just imagine how big SHE was.)

"Oh, you'll have fun," she said. "Come on, Daryll. You KNOW how often you've asked to stay alone. Why not build a mountain range? Or find a lake?"

The lake was a cheering thought. Like any baby, Daryll was particularly fond of water. What a wonderful mess he could make, all on his own!

"WE WON'T BE FAR," thundered his dad. "CALL IF YOU NEED US."

So Daryll hugged them both, and said goodbye.

The minute they were out of sight, he found a lake and jumped straight into it.

What a splash! Just think about it. Imagine a whole school going up into the air and coming down, CRASH, SPLASH! into a lake. High in the clouds, flying eagles got their stomachs wet, and wondered if it was raining, upside-down.

Soon, the water in the lake was all outside it. For miles around, there was nothing but squishy mud. Then, Daryll wallowed in the mud. There was no one to tell him not to. It was wonderful.

Time passed. In fact, a thousand years passed very quickly, while Daryll played. Before he was bored with mud, the squishy, flattish place had become a swamp, crawling with snakes and alligators. Coloured birds flew squawking from tree to tree.

Then he moved on. Just a bit further away, the sea began. To a sticky, mud-covered dragon, it looked delicious. He waded in, causing floods along the seashore. He washed all over, and floated for a while, just thinking.

Then, he had a really great idea. He dived deep down. With his great claws, he began to dig the seabed, piling enormous fistfuls of sand and mud into a wall. He was making a deep, wide hole, under the sea. He dived and dug, dived and dug, dived and dug.

When he finally stood up and looked around, the whole of the seashore looked completely different. The wall of sea mud joined the shore like a long, curved arm. Daryll had made a bay!

Outside the arm of the bay, the waves from the open sea still crashed and battered. But inside, the sea was still and sleepy. Already, groups of seals were bathing there.

Meanwhile, the bottom of the bay was now so deep that the little waves could hardly crawl up to the shore. Miles and miles of clean, new sand were showing. It was lovely. Daryll had made a beach.

Now, he was ready to try the mountain range. He had a plan.

As you know (though you may possibly have forgotten), dragons can fly. Daryll hadn't done it for a while, so he had to practice first. He flapped his wings, and ran until he got a good speed, and took off, wheeling around the sky until his wings felt nice and easy.

Then, as he flew, he put down his head and stretched his arms out like a swimmer, pointing his front claws straight ahead, like the teeth of a digger. Then he dived.

BBBRRRR!!!!!! Daryll's claws ploughed up the earth into a huge, great ditch. On either side, the earth piled up at speed. The air was filled with dirt and dust and flying boulders.

Daryll ploughed that ditch again and again. At either side, a row of hills began to grow – getting bigger and bigger, till they were twice as high as Daryll.

The ditch became a deep and narrow valley. The rows of hills began to grow into two mountain ranges.

Then, suddenly, there was a roar. Daryll looked back. A wall of water was rushing straight towards him!

Without knowing it, he had ploughed through the side of an underground lake. Now, the lake had burst into the narrow valley. Here it came, rushing down to the distant sea! Daryll scrambled out, just in time.

He had made a river!

He sat on one of the smaller of his hills, breathing hard until he had got his breath back. Then, he stretched out his ankles into the water. The water rushed over them, cold and tingly. It was gorgeous. His own shining, brand-new river!

Daryll was terribly excited now. And he was tired, too.

He wanted to SHOW somebody. He wanted his mum and dad.

"Now remember," his dad had said to him that morning. "Whenever you want us, you only have to call."

He didn't want to call. Why didn't they come for him? Why didn't they just KNOW that it was time!

He sulked. He sniffed. He felt forgotten. A great, big dragon tear rolled down his face, and hit the hill below.

But what had happened to that hill? Already, a forest had crept over it. Trees had grown up, halfway to his knees. It was beautiful.

"Dad!" called Daryll. "Mum! Come and see what I did! COME AND SEE!"

From far away, came a low, tremendous roar, like a growl of thunder. It was Daryll's dad, calling back to him, "WE'RE COMING, DARYLL!"

Thump, thump. The earth was trembling with their running footsteps. Birds went squawking, and the sky was darkening.

And look! There was his great, green, wonderful, frightful mother – a vast and shining lady dragon, as big as a mountain. Behind her was his enormous dragon father – I can't begin to say how big HE was.

Daryll leaped up onto his mother's back. Together the three of them looked at what he had made – his swamp, his beautiful bay, his shining river.

"WELL DONE, MY LAD!" thundered Daryll's father. The three of them hugged each other, and Daryll's father thumped his scaly back.

"And NOW," said Daryll's mother, "bath – and bed!"

They bathed in the sea until they felt all clean and fresh.

"What a lovely bay you made," said Daryll's mother. "Let's camp here tonight."

"WHY NOT?" thundered Daryll's dad.

For supper, they ate a forest or two, since they were vegetarian. Then they settled down. They stretched out

their tails into the cool, refreshing sea, and laid their heads on some convenient little hills. Their great bodies sank into the soft, deep sand of Daryll's beach as though it was an enormous feather bed.

"Now, isn't this nice?" said Daryll's mum.

"Mmm," said Daryll. He was almost asleep already.

Daryll's dad yawned an enormous yawn. He said, "What a day it's been! I could sleep for SEVEN THOUSAND YEARS!"

And they did.

The next time you go to the seashore, take a look. You might just see the three of them sleeping there.

# The Way Out

## JOYCE DUNBAR

Thompson was a long-haired hamster. He was very clean and very curious. He belonged to a boy called Luke.

Thompson's cage was in Luke's bedroom. It was a good-sized cage, with an upstairs and a downstairs. It had a newspaper nest inside a sleeping compartment, drinking water in a bottle on the side, a wheel and two ladders.

Thompson slept all day, but when night time came he was up and about. He ran around his cage, up and down his ladders, round and round in his wheel. But that wasn't enough.

Thompson wanted to find the way out.

One night, after Luke had gone to bed, Thompson saw that his cage door was open! Thompson stayed still for a minute, sat on his hind legs, smartened up his whiskers and listened. He could feel the big room all around him!

He scrambled through the open door and toppled onto the bedroom floor. Across the carpet he scuttled, under the bed, into the cupboard, along the shelves, in and out of shoes, in between Luke's toys. But that still wasn't enough.

Thompson wanted to find the way out.

So he gnawed at the skirting board and scraped at the floorboards. He sniffed at the gap by the door then managed to squeeze his way through. Thompson stayed still for a moment, pricked up his ears and listened. He could feel the big house all around him!

Through the bedrooms he ran, in and out of the bathroom, before scrambling all the way downstairs. He went into the living room, behind the sofa, in and out of drawers, under the door into the kitchen. Even so, that wasn't enough.

Thompson wanted to find the way out.

Then he smelt something through the cat-flap in the door. Fresh air! He flipped through onto the path outside. There he stayed still for a moment, took a deep breath and listened. He could feel the big town all around him!

Across the garden he ran, through the gate, all along the street, past the shops and schools, until he reached the middle of the town. Even so, that wasn't enough.

Thompson wanted to find the way out.

Then he saw a bus waiting at the bus-stop.

Thompson stayed still for a moment, cocked his head on one side and listened. He could sense the big country all around him!

So he stowed away on the bus and went through villages, towns and cities. He hopped on and off trains which took him up and down dale. He ran through forests and over fields until he came to the edge of the land. Yet still that wasn't enough.

Thompson wanted to find the way out.

Then he saw the wide open sea. Thompson sat still for a moment, polished his nose with his paws and listened. He could feel the great world all around him!

So he stowed away on a ship, to the North Pole and the South Pole. And he stowed away on aeroplanes to the East and to the West. Soon he had been right around the world! But it just wasn't enough.

Thompson wanted to find the way out.

He looked up at the great empty sky. Thompson sat still for a moment, heaved a big sigh and listened. He could feel outer space all above him!

So he stowed away on a rocket to the moon. He ran all around the moon, in and out of craters. Then he jumped onto a shooting star which took him to the edge of the universe.

He peeped over the edge of the universe. He saw an endless big black hole!

E-E-E-K!

Thompson had had quite enough. He wanted to find the way home.

Thompson sat still for a moment, stood on his hind legs and suddenly felt very dizzy. He covered his eyes with his paws and fell into the big black hole.

Down and down he went, very fast and far, until he landed with a very soft bump.

Thompson uncovered his eyes. He was back inside Luke's room.

"Where have you been?" cried Luke. "I've been looking everywhere for you!" Luke picked him up and stroked him and put him back inside his cage, with an upstairs and a downstairs and a wheel and two ladders.

Thompson sat still for a moment, then he had some biscuit for breakfast and a drink from his bottle. He smoothed down his fur and curled up in his newspaper nest.

How cosy and sleepy he felt! How very safe and sound!

# Baby Wizard

## CHRIS POWLING

Once there was a Baby Wizard.

Her Dad was a wizard, her Mum was a wizard and so was her big brother, aged five, who'd just started Wizard School. They lived in a spiky-towered castle with a deep, dark forest all round it – which is just where you'd expect a wizard family to live.

One thing you wouldn't expect, though. *This* Baby Wizard was special. She couldn't walk yet. She couldn't talk yet. She couldn't feed herself yet – and she certainly couldn't use her potty.

BUT SHE COULD MAKE MAGIC!

At first, of course, the family didn't believe it.

"Impossible," said her Dad. "Wizards must learn how to make magic – no one can be magical while they're still wearing a nappy!"

Baby Wizard could.

"Goo-goo-goo," she said. And instantly she turned

her pram into a racing car that roared straight down the motorway as far as the big city. Her Mum and Dad were furious when they had to collect her from the police station.

Mealtimes were even worse. Sometimes Baby Wizard turned her food into rubber so it bounced all over the castle kitchen. Sometimes she made it so heavy it fell to the floor with a CRASH that shook the whole forest. Sometimes she floated it out of the window, so it hung high over the castle like a tiny, food-coloured cloud.

At bathtimes she was even naughtier – filling the bath with crocodiles, for instance.

"Crocodiles?" shrieked Mum, snatching Baby Wizard from the water. "She's too little even to have heard of crocodiles!"

"Goo-goo-goo," said Baby Wizard. And the crocodiles changed into dragons so fiery they nearly

burnt the bathroom to bits with their breath.

Naturally, all this was a great nuisance – but nothing more than a nuisance. Remember, every member of her family was a wizard. They could always put things right with plenty of magic of their own.

The real problem came at bedtime.

Bedtime, yes.

Her Mum and Dad and her big brother, aged five, were too terrified now to go to sleep. Night after night they lay awake wondering what Baby Wizard would get up to after dark.

"Suppose it's a magic sneeze!" exclaimed her Dad. "She might blow away the whole forest!"

"Suppose it's a magic burp!" cried Mum. "She might split the castle in two like an earthquake!"

"Suppose it's a magic nightmare!" yelled her big brother, aged five. "She might fill every corner of the forest with gho-gho-gho-ghosts!"

Even when they took turns to watch over Baby Wizard's cot it didn't help. They were still so scared of what might happen none of them shut their eyes for a moment.

"This is terrible," yawned Baby Wizard's Mum. "I can't remember when we last had a good night's sleep."

"We're falling to bits from tiredness," Dad groaned. "Isn't there anything we can do?"

Baby Wizard's big brother, aged five, looked down at his little sister in her cot and scratched his head thoughtfully.

"Dad," he said. "Can a kitten do magic?"

"A kitten?"

"Or a puppy?"

"A puppy?"

"Or a chick? Or a calf? Or a piglet?"

"Of course not," Dad Wizard said. "Only a wizard can do magic – you learn how at Wizard School. Or so I thought till your sister came along."

"That's what I thought," said Baby Wizard's big brother, aged five. "So now I've got the answer to our problem!"

Quickly he waggled his fingers and muttered a magic word.

"Miaow-miaow-miaow," went Baby Wizard in her sleep. Then "purr-purr-purr".

Baby Wizard's big brother, aged five, had turned her into a kitten!

Every bedtime after that, Baby Wizard licked her whiskers, curled her tail and purred herself to sleep till morning . . . except, of course, when she'd been turned into a puppy or a chick or a calf or a piglet.

And her family slept happily ever after.

Especially her big brother, aged five, who'd just started Wizard School. Some people say that by the time he's grown up he'll be the best wizard ever . . . unless, of course, his sister is just as good.

# A Lullaby for Freddy

## ADÈLE GERAS

When Freddy the Fearless moved into the doll's house there was great excitement.

"He's a soldier," said Keith the little velvet frog. "I expect he'll have all kinds of stories to tell."

"He's bound to be tremendously brave," said Baby, the painted wooden doll who never moved from the wooden cradle.

"And strong," said Minna the rag doll. "Have you seen how tall and straight he stands in his shiny blue and gold uniform? And isn't that a sword strapped round his waist?"

Freddy the Fearless turned out to be every bit as brave and strong as Baby and Minna had hoped. He was also very talkative, just as Keith had said he would be.

"I expect," Freddy said, on the very first day, "that all of you are longing to hear tales of my soldiering, my bravery, assorted sagas of fights and battles and so on,

aren't you? I mean, this is an extremely pleasant doll's house, and they do say a change is as good as a rest, but it's not quite what I'm used to, oh no indeed!"

"Did you live in a barracks?" Minna wanted to know.

"In a fort," answered Freddy the Fearless, his voice full of pride. "A splendid cardboard fort in the middle of a sandy desert. There were palm trees and camels and we had battles in the morning. In the afternoon we marched around and had parades, and in the evening we all lined up on the floor of the fort for a spot of shut-eye. Oh, those were the days!"

"Where are all the other soldiers now?" Baby asked.

"Gone," said Freddy sadly. "Every last one. Dropped behind chests of drawers, exchanged for cars and things, taken away and given to jumble sales if there was anything wrong with them at all, even the slightest scratch . . . oh, there have been so many casualties!"

"Well, we lead a very quiet life here," said Keith. "In the daytime, sometimes we are played with and sometimes we aren't."

"What do you do when you're not being played with?" Fearless Freddy wanted to know.

"We chat," said Baby. "There's always plenty to chat about."

"Oh, I'm just the chap you need then," said Freddy. "I know wonderful stories. I'll keep you amused for hours."

And he did. The first day simply flew past, and Minna, Keith and Baby heard about the Adventure of the Dining-room Table, and the Battle of the Desk, when Freddy rode on the back of a wooden elephant through tropical jungles of pencil trees. Then there was the time when he fell into the basin and bobbed about in the water for a full ten minutes before being rescued.

Then the night time came, but it wasn't really dark in the doll's house. There were comforting patches of golden light from the landing which shone into the room and into the windows of the doll's house as well. Keith rested his head on one of his pink velvet legs and prepared to dream of waterlilies. Baby stared at the pattern in the ceiling and wondered what she could pretend it was tonight. Minna flopped into the corner and listened to the night noises.

"That's a strange sound," she said to herself. "It's just like someone crying. But Baby doesn't cry, and neither does Keith, and everyone knows that brave soldiers never, never cry. Who can it be?"

The snuffling went on and on, quite softly at first, and then louder and louder ... boo ... hoo ... boo ... hoo.

"Is that you, Baby?" Minna whispered.

"No," Baby said.

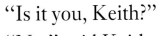

"Is it you, Keith?"

"No," said Keith. "You woke me up. I was dreaming of waterlilies."

"Is it you Fearless Freddy?"

"I'm afraid it is," came Freddy's voice out of the corner where he'd been put. "I'm sorry to say it is."

"But what's the matter?" asked Baby.

"I'm frightened."

"How can you be frightened?" Keith said. "There are no enemies here, and no battles. There isn't anything to be frightened of."

"Yes there is," said Freddy. "I'm frightened of the dark."

Minna, Baby and Keith thought about this for a moment.

"It isn't even properly dark," said Minna at last. "Look, there's a triangle of golden light shining through the door. Can you see?"

"But there are still dark corners," said Fearless Freddy. "And shadows. What's that, for instance? That big, square shadow just over there?"

"I expect it's my cradle," said Baby, "making a black patch on the wall."

"Isn't there anything we can do?" asked Keith. "What did you do in the fort?"

"Our general sang us a lullaby," said Freddy. "Only don't tell anyone I told you."

"And did that help you not to be scared of the dark?" Minna asked.

"Oh yes," said Freddy. "It had special words, but I can't remember what they are. If only I could remember, I'd be all right, I know I would."

"I know lots of lullabies," said Minna. "Every night I'll sing some of the lullabies I know and perhaps that will help."

"Good show!" said Freddy, not sounding in the least bit scared. "Sing away!"

So Minna sang Freddy all her very best and sleepiest-sounding special lullabies. Then she whispered, "Are you still frightened, Freddy?"

The only answer was the buzz of snores coming from Fearless Freddy's corner. He was fast asleep.

"He must be all right, after all," said Minna. "Goodnight everyone."

No one answered. Minna heard only the snuffles of a dreaming frog and the soft breathing of a baby in her cradle. She closed her eyes and went to sleep till morning.

*Hush-a-bye baby on the tree top.*
*When the wind blows the cradle will rock;*
*When the bough breaks, the cradle will fall;*
*Down will come baby, cradle and all.*

# When Am I
# Going Home?

## SALLY GRINDLEY

Christopher's bed was right under the window. Sanjit's bed was on one side and Alice's was on the other. Christopher had been in hospital longer than Sanjit and Alice, and he was very fed up with lying in bed all day long.

"When am I going home?" he asked his mum every morning.

"When you're better," said his mum.

"When will that be?" he asked.

"Soon," said his mum. "Try to be patient."

But sometimes soon can seem like a very long time.

Christopher 's favourite nurse was Nurse Ball. She was short and round and bouncy, just like a ball, and she always found time to spend with the children.

"You look in a right-down-in-the-dumps-misery-me sort of mood today," she said one morning.

"I'm bored," said Christopher, "and fed up, and I hate lying in this rotten old bed all day long."

"Rotten old bed!" exclaimed Nurse Ball, looking thoroughly shocked. "I'll have you know that's a magic bed you're lying in, young man."

"Don't be silly," said Christopher. "It's a rotten, old, hard hospital bed and I hate it."

"You mark my words," said Nurse Ball, "if you believe it's a magic bed, then a magic bed it will be. And magic beds can turn into anything and go anywhere you want them to."

"I don't believe you," Christopher laughed.

Nurse Ball just winked.

In the afternoon, after he had seen all the doctors and eaten his lunch, and before his dad came to visit, Christopher lay wishing something exciting would happen. He remembered what Nurse Ball had said about his bed and grinned. Part of him was sure that she was just pulling his leg, but another part of him thought how much fun he could have if only his bed were really magic. All the places he could go to ... All the things it could become ... Imagine whizzing through the air ... Imagine ...

Suddenly, he was at the wheel of a fire engine which was screaming along a road, siren blaring – NEE NA, NEE NA, NEE NA.

"Out of the way, idiot!" yelled Sanjit, who was sitting beside him, to the driver of a yellow car that was blocking the road. NEE NA, NEE NA, NEE NA.

In front of them they could see masses of black smoke billowing up into the sky, and bright orange flames dancing at the windows and skipping along the roof of an old warehouse. The fire engine screeched to a halt and Christopher and Sanjit jumped down. Other fire engines were already there, and the Fire Chief shouted at them to hurry up. They rushed towards the warehouse and directed their hoses at the burning windows. The heat from the flames knocked them back. It was scorching. Too hot to bear . . .

"Christopher, it's time for your medicine," a familiar voice came from close by. "What've you been up to, young man? You've got yourself all hot and bothered."

"I've been fighting a fire," said Christopher excitedly.

"Ah," said Nurse Ball. "I told you it was a magic bed."

Christopher's bed took him into the operating theatre the next day, and he didn't remember much after that.

But a few days later, when he was feeling much better and wishing he could go on another adventure, it took him across the world to see the elephants in Africa. It became a safari jeep which bumped and rattled its way through the parched savannah scrub.

"Look at those zebras!" yelled Alice above the noise.

"And there's a giraffe over there!" shouted Sanjit from the back.

As they drove through the next tangled mass of dusty bushes, they suddenly saw a large herd of elephants drinking at a small water hole.

"Wow!" said Christopher. "Just look at that huge mother elephant!"

"And look at the little baby one!" cried Alice. "I didn't know they could be so tiny."

"They're wonderful," said Sanjit.

It was Nurse Ball who drove away the elephants.

"You were miles away, Christopher. Another adventure?"

"I've just seen the elephants in Africa. They're beautiful."

"They certainly are," said Nurse Ball. "You're a lucky young man to have seen them. What's more, I've

good news for you. Your temperature's coming down, which means you're on the mend."

"Yippee!" yelled Christopher. "Does that mean I'm going home soon?"

"Just a little while longer," smiled Nurse Ball. "You might fit in one or two more adventures before you go. But don't tire yourself out."

Christopher's bed didn't stay still over the next two weeks. Every day, as soon as the doctors had examined him and after he had eaten his lunch, Christopher set off on a new adventure. His bed became a bulldozer and knocked over an old building. It flew him to Disney World to meet Mickey Mouse and Donald Duck. It drove him to school to visit all the friends he was missing while he was in hospital. It turned into a boat and took him deep sea fishing in the middle of the night. And it took him all the way to Scotland to eat crumpets in front of the fire with his grandparents.

Then, one afternoon, the bed became a hot air balloon. It was a beautiful day, the sun shining and clouds racing across the sky in the warm breeze. The pink, purple and red balloon swelled and swayed as Christopher filled it with the blasts of hot air that would raise it from the ground.

And they were off! Up and up! Higher and higher! Carried by the wind across the sky. Down below everything grew smaller and smaller until the cars looked like Christopher's toys and the houses like doll's houses.

"I can see my house!" yelled Christopher, "and look, there's my dad in the garden."

"My house is over there," yelled Alice. "The one with the red roof."

"And there's mine," shouted Sanjit, "just there by the park."

"I'm going to go home," said Christopher. "I'm going to go home. I'm going to go and see my mum and dad. Let's take the balloon down. Won't they be surprised?"

Christopher was fast asleep when his mum and dad came to see him at the hospital later that afternoon. They quietly packed his clothes into a bag and gently carried him to the car. When he woke up he found himself tucked up in his own bed in his own bedroom.

"Welcome home, son," said his delighted parents.

"So it really was a magic bed!" exclaimed Christopher. "Nurse Ball was right!"